Bone Island Bodies

A Brody Wahl Mystery Novelette

Wayne Gales

To the lost, the hurt, the lonely, the abused, and
the misunderstood.

1 Charley

I barely had my pen down when Lucy, my boss's secretary, poked her head around the doorframe. Late afternoon sunlight streaked through the blinds, striping the carpet in gold. "Charley, Mr. Long wants to see you before you go."

I forced a neutral smile, hoping for a five-second question rather than a full meeting. A frosty beer waited for me at Twin Peaks on International Drive—its chilled promise like a siren call in my mind. After twenty years with FDLE Orlando, I'd grown accustomed to running cases solo. My ninety-percent arrest record practically guaranteed I could chase clues wherever I pleased without interruptions.

Long's office reeked of stale coffee and aged leather. He indicated the chair in front of his heavy oak desk, then clicked the door shut behind me. The room felt suddenly smaller.

"I'm assigning you TDY— temporary duty— with the Monroe County Sheriff' s Office down in the Keys," he said, tapping a stack of papers. " You were born in Key West, and I hear you still go back often." His thin smile twisted like a knife-edge. "Sometimes I don't think the locals know how to untangle their own messes."

He slid yesterday's Key West Citizen across the blotter. I peered at the headline, bold enough to stop my heart for a moment: THIRD BODY IN A MONTH FOUND. The subheadline spelled out every gory detail: three mature males in their sixties, two recovered by recreational divers bobbing over pale reefs, the third dumped roadside like garbage. No fingerprints match any database. No DNA but the victims' own.

I swallowed. "Why me?" I said, folding the paper in my hands until the ink left smudges on my fingertips. It felt heavier than the file folders and case binders I normally carried. "I get the geography, but what do old men with broken bodies have to do with sexual assault?"

Long leaned back, face grim. "That's why I closed the door." He flicked on his desk lamp, pushing the afternoon into shadow. "The sheriff's office did release that the victims were mutilated, but kept the most disturbing facts under wraps. I want you there to keep it that way until we catch whoever did this."

He opened a lower drawer and produced a manila envelope thicker than two. Inside lay eight-by-ten black-and-white photos. I lifted the top print and felt bile rise in my throat. Three ash-white faces stared up from the glossy surface, eyes wide in eternal terror, mouths stuffed with dark, indiscernible masses.

Even Long's usual composure cracked. His cheeks flushed, his throat working once before he nodded silently. I studied the second and third photos, each more grotesque than the last, and wondered exactly what I'd agreed to leave my beer—and my comfort zone—behind for.

Old Bahia Honda Bridge

2 Brody

Broderick Russell Wahl pressed himself flat against the back wall of the half-rusted shark cage, fifty feet beneath the churning surface of Florida Bay. Sunlight, fractured into greenish beams by the turbid water, danced across the moss-encrusted pillars of the Bahia Honda Bridge overhead. With a cool, practiced motion, he dipped his grease pencil against the little waterproof slate bolted to the cage's inside. Thirteen checkmarks now—twelve hammerheads, six bull sharks, one blacktip reef shark, two sluggish nurse sharks—each tally as mundane to him as counting barnacles on a pier piling. He felt only a mild tightening in his chest when he glanced toward the deep current, knowing the bulls' hulking silhouettes could materialize without warning.

He had sparred with Florida Fish and Wildlife for days, arguing that a man who'd lived half his life among sharks needed no steel bars to feel safe. Yet as he studied the small knots of hammerheads weaving with curious precision, and the lumbering nurse sharks sulking in the shadows, he conceded the cage was more than mere insurance. A hammerhead's bite might be an accidental brush of denticles; a bull's attack was unmistakably predatory, a deliberate, lunch-time strike that left no room for negotiation.

Even so, the slate of predators before him did little to still the storm in his mind. His thoughts drifted, as they had all week, to the letter tucked into the pocket of his wetsuit jacket—a letter he'd read a dozen times, each word etched into his memory with laser-sharp clarity. He pictured the familiar looping script:

My Dearest Brody,

I hope the turquoise currents of Key West find you well this summer. I can almost see you now—mask on, fins kicking, the thrill of unknown depths calling your name. The twins are thriving at Kibbutz Ein Gev, learning Hebrew the same way they mastered your sea stories—by diving in headfirst. Their laughter echoes across the Sea of Galilee, a promise that home can be anywhere love abides.

I must tell you something that may sadden you: I've chosen to stay here in Israel. Partly to be near our children, but mostly because I've discovered a purpose that demands all of my heart—and the endowment left to me by my godfather. There are refugees by the millions—hungry, unvaccinated, dying in the deserts of Africa and the tents of the Middle East. They are mostly strangers of different faiths, but I refuse to view their prayers as anything less than cries for mercy. I know this path will be fraught with danger, resistance, even violence from those who wield suffering as power—but I cannot turn away.

I'm not leaving our marriage, and I will never stop loving you. Yet I cannot wait in Key West while the world burns around me. I still love you, Brody, but I do not love who I have become here. I hope time will show us both where our destinies truly lie.

Always,

Mallory

His chest tightened, as though a current of longing dragged him deeper than any ocean trench. Mallory's words were kind but precise—no promises of return, no invitation to follow. Just the quiet, resolute closing of one chapter and the opening of another, unshared by him.

He forced his gaze back outward, toward the slate, toward the circling teeth around him. The cable slack in his gloved hand felt like the only lifeline to reality. He was about to tug the signal rope—two strong jerks to the crew on the skiff overhead—when movement at the edge of his vision froze him in place. The murk cleared for a moment, and

Brody watched as a dozen sharks converged in a spinning mass, heads darting, tails flicking in a rare feeding frenzy. Bull Sharks and Hammerheads sliced through the swirl like scythes, and a few enormous cobia hovered on the fringes, feasting on scraps too small for the pelagic predators.

Somewhere in that churning ballet lay the source of the commotion, but he couldn't make it out. The tide's push and pull blurred the outlines. He fought the urge to yank the rope and surface to reset his tank. Curiosity—ancient and hungry—kept his arm still.

Then, as if choreographed, a single bull shark peeled away from the pack, gliding straight to him. In its jaws was a shape pale and rigid, drifting like flotsam on the tide. Brody's heart pounded so fiercely he thought the cage would shudder. Even through the regulator's mouthpiece, he formed the word "wow," a sound too small for the vast silence. The creature dropped its prize in the sand-stirred gloom. Brody exhaled slowly and raised a finger to his mask's skirt—an impossible question on his lips. When he leaned forward to peer into the gloom, the pale form resolved into the unmistakable outline of a human leg.

3 Charley

The Lieutenant slid a glossy eight-by-ten photograph across the cold, steel desk. Under the harsh fluorescent lights, the image glowed with sickly clarity: a close-up of a man's mutilated groin. "Their penis and testicles," Long said flatly, watching me absorb the horror. "All three victims had their genitals sheared off with almost surgical precision, then stuffed down their throats." He leaned forward, voice low: "Toxicology on the stomach contents shows traces of dark-roast coffee and enough phenobarbital to fell a horse."

I lifted the photo, feeling its weight in my fingers, then handed it back. Long dropped it gently into a manila envelope and set it beside a stack of files. "They choked to death," he went on. "No apparent struggle, and get this— every drop of blood was drained from their bodies. No blood spatter, no trail. It's as if they bled out into thin air."

My lips thinned. After ten years investigating sex crimes—runaways, exploited girls, murdered co-eds—this was the first time I'd been called in for the murder of men. "Any other details?" I asked, leaning back against the edge of the desk.

Long flipped through his notes, the pages crackling. "All victims were small men—five-nine or under, slight build. Each had deep contusions along the spine, like they'd been dragged across rough metal, maybe a car trunk." He paused, brows knitting. "Two more things: all three were registered sex offenders. They'd served their time years ago, kept clean, maintained parole, living off the grid. And we've got two missing persons who fit the same profile—under five-seven, with criminal records. I doubt it's a coincidence. Whoever's doing this is playing vigilante. Registered-offender registries are public; Key West is crawling with targets."

Long snapped his notebook shut. "Can you leave tomorrow? I'll book your flight and rental car."

I managed a wry half-smile. "I hate flying, rental cars, and hotels. Let me take my unmarked service unit—reliable, inconspicuous. I'll drive straight through and crash with friends. No telling who's been on a hotel bedspread." I stood. "I'll pack up and head south this afternoon. They need help sooner rather than later."

He shrugged, sliding the envelope of photos and a heavy folder of forensic and police reports to me

. "Suit yourself," he said. "Here's who to call in Key West." I tucked the files under my arm and strode out, already plotting the long highway south and the darkness waiting at the end of it.

4 Brody

It took barely fifteen minutes for the morning's tranquil nature study in the Keys to morph into a full-blown crime scene. The sun glared off the turquoise water as traffic ground to a halt in both directions on the Bahia Honda bridge, cars idling bumper to bumper like reluctant tourists. Brody sat on a folding chair parked against a patrol SUV, sweat beading at his temples, while deputies in crisp uniforms peered over the railings, scanning for any sign of… whatever had happened below.

Sheriff's Deputy Jacob Sands—broad-shouldered, sun-leathered, with the salt-streaked patch of Florida Fish and Wildlife on his sleeve—strode across the asphalt, barking instructions to the FWC crew as they hauled a steel shark cage from the skiff onto the bridge. When he reached Brody, the deputy's boots kicked up little puffs of dust. Sands had known Brody's father, Bric Wahl, for decades—had watched Brody himself grow from a lanky kid in flippers into a razor-sharp diver and treasure hunter.

"Brody," Sands said, voice low but urgent, "we're flat out of divers today. We need to position this cage right over that spot you marked—where you saw the feeding activity— and retrieve anything down there before it sinks or drifts away." He paused, letting the humid breeze carry his words. "I'm authorized to bring you on as a contract diver for Monroe County Sheriff's."

Sands ran a sunburnt hand through his hair, cracked a wry smile. "Our last guy up and quit a few months back— ran off to some ski resort in Breckenridge to swing a hammer in the snow. I told him to enjoy bein' buried up to his balls in powder, then waved him goodbye."

He looked Brody square in the eye. "I never dared hire your old man—too many gray areas in his record—but you, you've got the skill and no tarnished reputation. How'd you

13

like a semi-full-time gig? Most days it's recovering stolen scooters or wrecked cars, maybe an old plane fuselage. We leave the big narcotics stuff to the Coast Guard—unless they botch a traffic stop on US-1."

Brody felt something tighten in his chest. Two job offers in four days, and this one came with salt water and steel cages—home turf. He thought of her: Would she have stayed if I'd been working? Probably not. Just another excuse, he realized.

Without shaking Sands's hand, Brody tipped his head in a curt nod. Implicit acceptance. Details like hours or pay were secondary—he was in.

"All right," Sands said, stepping back with a grin. "Suit up. We've got evidence to pull from the depths."

Brody's mouth twisted into a grim half-smile. "Evidence? By the time we haul that cage into position, there won't be enough left to sponge off. The big predators will take their fill, then the little scavengers will pick the bones clean. Whatever's left of that poor bastard will be shark shit in two hours flat."

5 Charley

Depending on the hour, the ride from Orlando to Key West stretches between six and eight hours. Once I've slogged through the sameness of the turnpike—endless lanes of gray asphalt and the distant hum of truck engines— my spirits lift as soon as I clear the seventeen-mile causeway from Florida City. The salt-laced wind off Biscayne Bay tugs at my hair, and the roadway narrows into a ribbon of sunshine and sea, leading me into Key Largo's lush mangroves and turquoise horizons.

Cruising down A1A, I can't help but mark each milepost and familiar landmark—the peeling green sign at mile marker eighty-one, the cluster of rum-shack stands just past Tavernier, even the dull shine of the occasional Monroe County Sheriff's cruiser. If I ever got pulled over, I'd flash that badge of mine and be on my way—though it's always easier to keep rolling than to explain "official business" at a roadside stop. I smirk every time I pass that ancient squad car in Layton: paint chipped to bare metal, windows streaked with grime, the sagging headliner half-collapsed inside. It fools no one—except maybe some wide-eyed tourist who's never seen a derelict island patrol car before.

I may have stretched the truth to my boss: I told him I was bunking with friends in Key West. In reality, I stay with Lillian Albury—Lilly—the one true constant in my life. Key West is in her blood: generations of Conchs stretching back through the Bahamas to the Carolinas and even to Mother England in the 1600s. More than a friend, she's my lover, my anchor, my reason I'd drop everything in Central Florida and move back here in a heartbeat.

Lilly's house sits on Linda Street in New Town, walled in by eight-foot brick that shields a shaded oasis: a gleaming pool, a bubbling jacuzzi, and a private patio tangled with orchids and bougainvillea. No need for swimsuits—day or night, we're both perfectly comfortable au naturel. Best of all, there's a two-car garage, a rare luxury on the crowded island.

I didn't call ahead. She loves surprises. Rolling up her driveway, I clicked the garage opener, let the door rise, and drove in. I stripped off my clothes in the cool concrete gloom, slipped through the back door, and stepped naked into the lush backyard. The air smelled of damp tile and blooming jasmine. Before I could exhale, Lilly's Vietnamese pot-bellied pig—Man—scuttled over, snorting with delight at the treats he knows I bring.

I followed his little trot to the hot tub. There she was, reclining in the jet-whispered water under strung fairy lights, skin gleaming, a half-full wine glass balanced on the tub's rim and a second bottle chilling in a bucket. Anticipating my arrival, she lifted her glass in a playful toast. "You know where the glasses are, honey. And grab that extra cabernet on the counter—been a two-bottle kind of day." Her voice was low, amused.

Inside the open-air kitchen I found the corkscrew in its usual spot and popped the dark red cab. I reached for an unbreakable acrylic ginormous wine glass, then turned to the candy dish perched by the fruit bowl. She knew exactly what I wanted: pure, white, full-strength Oxycodone. I scooped a fistful into my palm, rolled them into my mouth, and washed them down with wine. Man grunted indignantly, nosing at my pockets in hopes of a handout. I wagged a finger at him. "No, pig—these are bad for you." *(I reminded myself the same was true for me.)* I snagged another handful and carried them back to the tub.

Lilly parted her lips, so I tossed in half a dozen, letting them clink into the water, then swallowed the rest. I had no doubt she'd already polished off her share and was edging toward a delicious, floating haze. Man stood at the tub's lip, bristling expectantly, and I scratched behind his ear as Lilly stretched, head tipped back beneath the fairy lights. I laughed and asked, "Why'd you name him Man?"

Her eyes darkened in that soft island dusk. "Because all men are pigs," she said quietly. I chuckled—then saw a flicker of hurt. I cleared my throat. "Tough day?" I leaned in for a lingering kiss.

"Brutal," Lilly sighed. As a nurse at the Florida Keys Medical Center, she's been stretched thin: too few staff, endless weekend traumas—drunk-driver wrecks, mopeds slammed by tourist SUVs, domestic-abuse cases, and the lurking burden of Covid. The Lower Keys aren't a maelstrom of violence, but with so few clinics, every accident feels magnified.

She nestled closer and said, "I'm so happy you came. I didn't expect you for another week. Miss me?" Her voice held a shaky giggle.

"Official business," I murmured, wrapping an arm around her. "And a bit of pleasure. I've been assigned to investigate the murders."

She stiffened, eyes flicking away. "Oh. Those," she said with a small, pained wince.

6 Brody

Brody Wahl wandered in a daze from his weathered houseboat in Garrison Bight onto Duval Street, the sun's slanting rays turning the pastel storefronts to molten candy. He had no destination in mind— only the urgent need to escape his floating refuge, where the relentless replay of that gruesome vision in Spanish Harbor still clawed at his thoughts. He wasn't easily rattled— he'd seen gunfire send men crumpling, felt a bullet tear through his side, even stared down sharks circling a lifeboat—but to witness a body torn limb from limb, piece by horrified piece, was a horror he could not shake.

Since Mallory and his father had packed up and left the big Key West house on Shark Key, Brody had been back on the boat, hoping water and wind would wash away the ache of family fracture. Their grand plan to buy a seaside home, with his father installed as a pampered permanent guest, unraveled within days of moving in. Mallory's vegan menus and strict "no-alcohol under this roof" decree stiffened his father's nerves, but it was her ban on overnight female visitors that truly broke him. Within three weeks Russell "Bric" Wahl vanished—first to a ramshackle mobile home on Geiger Key, then to an upstairs apartment over the old Hunks restaurant, claiming the lure of late-night company and a stiff drink outweighed caution or cellular paranoia.

After a quarter-hour of aimless trudging—dodging drunks, T-shirt hawkers, brazen timeshare pitchmen and the sizzle of buskers' steel drums—Brody found himself before the faded sign of Hunks. The tug of old habits drew him inside. He slid between a cluster of stools, the polished mahogany bar cool beneath his palms. From his shirt pocket he extracted Mallory's letter—edges softened by repeated folding, ink blurred where tears had fallen—and read it yet again, the same gentle words promising peace and a new beginning that somehow felt like a goodbye carved in paper.

Out of the corner of his glassy vision, Kevin Montclaire—known as Scarlett when the wig, corset, and rhinestones were in place—watched him. At six-five and pushing three hundred pounds, Kevin was a mountain of kindness in black leather, his arm tattoos peeking from beneath rolled sleeves. After ten silent minutes, he lifted a tall glass from behind the bar, filled it with ice pulsing condensation down the sides, and poured in dark, fizzing diet cola. He slid it across the lacquer to Brody with a soft "The usual?"

Brody caught the glass, raised it halfway to his lips, then set it back down with deliberate calm. He met Kevin's concerned gaze and managed a small, rueful smile. "Kevin," he said, voice low against the hum of neon and chatter, "I'm thirty-one. Don't you think it's time I grew up a little?"

Kevin's brow lifted, uncertainty mixing with sympathy in his dark eyes. He'd seen where this road had led Bric Wahl—sweet highs shadowed by crushing lows—but he recognized the hunger in Brody's tone, the craving for something stronger than cola.

Brody let silence stretch, then nodded. "All right. Make me a Mojito. I hear they're pretty tasty." And in that moment, he chose to taste something new.

Bone Island Bodies

7 Charley

Monday morning light crept over Cudjoe Key as I arrived at the squat, weathered Sheriff's Office, its peeling mint-green paint dulled by spray from the Gulf. Humid air clung to my shirt as I stepped inside the cramped lobby, where a single ceiling fan labored against the humidity. I signed in, then made the same pilgrimage down the highway to the Key West Police Station— two law-enforcement bodies squabbling over the same string of grisly discoveries. The victims hailed from Key West, but each corpse had turned up dumped in some lonely stretch of county road, leaving everyone eager to point fingers.

Deputy Jacob Sands met me in the sheriff's back office. He was a portly man in his early sixties, salt-and-pepper hair combed back carefully, his uniform crisp for a man a month from retirement. After introductions, he insisted on escorting me to Key West, as if the solemn glow of that station's fluorescent lights somehow bestowed higher authority. In the narrow police conference room, we watched red and blue flashes from patrol cars through the window. For twenty minutes I stood with arms folded, listening to two captains bicker about jurisdiction—voices rising until I finally let my palm crash against the laminate table. The clack echoed through the room.

"Gentlemen," I said, voice low but firm, "this isn't a pissing contest. My jurisdiction covers all of Florida. You do your job. I'll do mine." I snapped open my battered leather briefcase and laid out a thin stack of photographs and case notes. "This is everything I was given. What else have you found?"

Sands ran his hands over his uniform trousers in frustration. "Not much. Three bodies so far, two more still missing. All old men, stripped naked and left beside A1A or washed up along mangrove-lined shorelines. Wallets placed neatly within reach—almost like a taunt." He paused, as though recalling something more disturbing. "One victim had a rounded bruise on the back of his head. Not violent trauma—maybe a stumble. And the mouths… well, they were anal-ty with their own genitals shoved inside. Pale as damp plaster, not a drop of blood on the scene or the bodies. Forensic lab in Miami traced their lungs to chlorinated water—pool water, presumably. No prints, no fibers, no DNA except the victims themselves. Zero leads." He let out a long breath. "What kind of sick bastard does this?"

I leaned forward, brushing a stray curl from my brow. "Serial killers usually prey on women. A handful have targeted men—often young, often gay. Gacy murdered dozens of young men for no apparent reason; Dahmer killed seventeen, dismembered them, even consumed them. But the absolute lack of blood here… and the ritualized humiliation… That screams something more organized— could be a gang or a cult."

For the next few weeks I prowled Key West's neon-lit streets well past midnight: Duval Street pulsing with reggae hum, the scent of Key lime pie mingling with salt air, my rented Mustang rumbling over creaking wooden sidewalks. At dawn I'd return to my hideaway with Lilly—my partner, a junior night nurse with jasmine-scented skin—where we'd collapse into silk sheets and make love until sunlight slanted through the blinds. We'd sleep through the humid mornings, meet once more with the frustrated deputies in the early afternoon, then set out again under moonrise. Lilly traded shifts so she could share this fugue of lust and exhaustion. I'd be lying if I said I minded the routine—until I remembered I was here to catch a killer, not take a vacation.

As days slipped by, the county leads dried up. Someone plastered "$10,000 REWARD" flyers on telephone poles, carefully omitting any mention of mutilation to deter the crazies from hogging the hotline. Still, the phone never rang with anything useful—just crackpots accusing neighbors of

Martians hidden on Stock Island by "them," whoever "they" might be.

Three weeks later my cell lit up with a dispatch from the Monroe County office on Cudjoe Key: they'd found another body, same mutilation, same shocking pallor. This time on Little Torch Key, a lonely mile north of U.S. 1, where the coroner's van sat under swaying palms, and patrol cars formed a silent cordon. I parked, pulled on nitrile gloves, and crouched beside the corpse. The noonday sun bared every waxy crease in the skin, confirming the victim had indeed been bled dry. His lips gaped, jaw slack, the stiffening rigor mortis locking him halfway between gasp and resignation.

"No lividity," I murmured, straightening and peeling off my gloves with a crisp snap. "Looks like you're right—almost nothing left but a shell." I zipped my jacket and turned toward my car. "Send me the coroner's full report as soon as it's ready. I'm heading back into town—got a lead to chase." I climbed into the driver's seat before anyone could reply, the engine's growl replacing the cicadas' drone as I pulled away, racing the sun back toward Key West and whatever answers lay waiting there.

8 Flashback

Lillian Albury was six years old the first time she noticed how different Key West could be in the late 1970s. Her bright dress fluttered around her knees as she chased her Labrador retriever, Rocky, across the bleached-white sand of Dog Beach. Salt spray stung her eyes, and the sun baked the shells into a mosaic beneath her toes. Stray dogs padded in to join their family companions, tongues lolling, tails high in greeting. From October through April, the island teemed with tourists, their rental cars and sunburned families elbowing the narrow streets, but in summer the sweltering heat sent visitors scuttling away, leaving only the locals— and children like Lilly— to claim the shoreline.

Back then, Duval Street wasn't a gauntlet of souvenir shops and tiki-bar hawkers. Between Duval and Bahama Village, pastel clapboard houses sat quiet behind hedges, and banks, gas stations, and the old Kress department store lined the broad avenues. On Duval's west end, Shorty's Diner beckoned with its red vinyl booths and sizzling griddles; the air smelled of frying bacon and strong coffee. Or, if they craved burgers, neighbors piled into the Royal Castle on Roosevelt Boulevard, grease glistening on paper-wrapped patties. At night, Jimmy Buffett—still just a lone guitar player in the Chart Room—wove melodies about salt and sunshine, oblivious that soon he'd become a global legend. And Mel Fisher had yet to haul the Atocha's treasure from the seabed.

Lilly's father, a steady hand in her young world, died suddenly of a heart attack just as summer's haze settled in. Her mother, ten generations of Conch blood running in her veins, closed the shutters and wept for days. But six months later, on a humid evening inside the Wharf Rat bar, she met Stu. He was trim and athletic, salt-and-pepper hair combed neatly, and his easy laugh echoed off the sticky hardwood floor. By the time the jukebox had played a dozen songs, they were inseparable. They slipped away to Miami one morning, married by a Justice of the Peace in a pastel-walled chapel, then toasted their honeymoon with ice-cold vodka at the Fontainebleau. Behind them, Lilly watched from Grandma's front porch, arms folded over her chest.

Grandma Nelly Albury—stout of figure, lifelong keeper of Albury traditions—took Lilly into her 150-year-old Old Town home. Its shutters swung on rusting hinges, and the attic smelled of cedar trunks and mothballs. Lilly imagined secret tea parties beneath lace tablecloths in corners where sunbeams fell through dusty windows. She and her cousins tumbled through the overgrown backyard, shrieking to scare the lizards hiding in the weeds. But six months later, Grandma joined Lilly's father in the silent rows of the cemetery, leaving the child adrift in a world of polished floors and strangers' laughter.

With Grandma gone, Lilly's mother answered a help-wanted ad and took a cashier's post at Fast Buck Freddie's, the new variety store in the old Kress building on Duval. The cash register rang sharp as church bells all day long. Concerned for her daughter, she was grateful when Stu volunteered to spend his days off with Lilly.

"We'll go to Dog Beach," he promised in that cheerful voice, "or the park. Maybe even White Street Pier. Ice cream, shops—just you and me." Lilly shrugged as he pointed out her swimsuit and flip-flops, but inside she clenched her fists.

A few weeks later, Stu eased her resistance. He bought Lilly a pale blue two-piece swimsuit trimmed with ruffles—priceless in her seven-year-old mind. He praised her in that warm, steady tone: "You look beautiful, Lilly." Her cheeks bloomed pink. Their afternoon swims became routine: sandcastles, seaweed crowns, the soft slap of waves against Little Palm Island in the distance.

Then one afternoon, back at the house, she heard Stu's voice call through her bedroom door: "Fausto's ice cream? Want to go?" Without waiting for an answer, he pushed the door open. Lilly stood in the middle of the room, towel wrapped tight around her, and froze. Stu's lean frame was bare, pale under the ceiling fan's flicker, and a tension coiled in his eyes.

Later, in the living room, Stu crouched by Rocky, scratching between the old dog's ears while hot guilt pulled Lilly's stomach into tight knots. "This stays between us," he murmured, voice low. "Or something bad could happen to Rocky." The Labrador's gentle eyes blinked as Stu's hand tightened on the collar. "Some men bet on dogfights. Your friend here could fetch twenty-five dollars—if he survives four minutes in the ring." Rocky whimpered. Lilly dropped to her knees and wrapped her arms around him. "I won't tell," she sobbed. "Please don't hurt him."

Her visits with Stu became a nightmare repeated—each time her mother slipped out the door for work, each time his smile turned hollow and his hands grew cold. At the dinner table, Lilly pushed peas around her plate until they rolled off the edge. Her laughter vanished; her skin grew pinched and pale beneath her sundresses. Words stuck in her throat.

One summer morning, Rocky—old and gray around the muzzle—didn't bark at the front gate. Lilly discovered him lying still on the living room rug, his warm weight gone. She sank beside him, cried until her tears left her throat raw and silent. Then she lifted her eyes to Stu's drawn face. In that moment he saw her truth: she could no longer be controlled. His lips quivered, but he said nothing.

Fear pressed against her chest as Lilly realized her silence had ended. She imagined her mother's tender face when she spoke, the betrayal, the shock—and then guilt stopped the words on her tongue. What if Stu denied everything? What if he twisted the story against her? So

Lilly shoveled the memories deep into herself and said nothing.

In the years that followed, her mother remarried and eventually grew old; the long-concealed shame festered in Lilly's heart. When Nelly died and left the New Town house to her, Lilly returned home for the funeral. The hot Florida sun beat down on the churchyard as she spotted Stu standing by the rusted wrought-iron fence. Her throat tightened. She stepped forward, raised a trembling finger, and pressed it into his chest. Her voice dropped to a hiss. "I'll be home by dark. You have three hours to get out. If you don't, I'll kill you in your sleep."

Stu's face drained of color. He stumbled back, voice caught in his throat, and that night he drove away in silence. Lilly watched until his taillights vanished around the corner. She never spoke of those three years to another soul—but in the hush of every ocean breeze, she heard Rocky's soft approach, and she remembered

Wayne Gales

9 Brody

The job with the Monroe County Sheriff's Office proved every bit as dull as Officer Sands warned. Brody spent his first two weeks holed up on his weathered houseboat, the gentle slap of saltwater against old wood his only companion. He'd prop his phone on the steering console, watch its blank screen and listen for the rush of seagrass in the current, waiting—always waiting— for a call about a big case.

But the calls never came. Day by day, his anticipation drained away like the tide, replaced by a restless itch for real adventure and a newly acquired fondness for rum. One sweltering afternoon, unable to bear another idle minute, he shoved off his boat shoes, hoisted himself into a pair of khaki shorts, and followed his curiosity— and the promise of a cold drink— down Duval Street.

The humid air vibrated with the sound of steel drums, the scent of conch fritters, and the sweet tang of spilled beer. He passed the neon glow of Sloppy Joe's and the salty tang of Hog's Breath, intending to grab a plain old burger, maybe two, if hunger struck. But like a ship drawn to a siren's call, when he reached Hunks—its sign a haze of pink and blue neon—Brody drifted in as though sleepwalking. Electric bass pulsed through the air, neon beads of sweat dripped from the ceiling fans, and he murmured to himself, "One little drinky won't hurt. It's a Tuesday night—no calls tonight."

Inside, the air tasted of rum and citrus, the bar stools worn smooth by decades of elbows. Brody's eyes flicked over the crowd, scanning for his father, Bric Wahl— legendary diver, grizzled at seventy-one with a limp that told of gunshots and knife fights. He'd wanted to share news: his new badge, his newfound thirst for Mojitos, and pick his dad's brain about the nearly mythical way he'd charmed every woman in Key West, whether single or blissfully ignorant of her partner's proximity. When the usual table sat empty, Brody slid onto the stool at the very end of the bar, where he could nurse a drink and keep half an eye on any unattached tourists.

His spirits sagged—until he saw Bric round the corner of Duval, cane tapping on the brick. Brody's chest tightened with pride; the old man's sea-weathered face creased into a grin. Holding his half-empty glass aloft, Brody bellowed, "Dad!" The mint and lime stirred in his cup as he waved like a fool. Bric cocked his head, surprise flickering in his pale blue eyes, then pushed back the door and joined him.

Kevin, the big black bartender in the corner, slid Bric a dark, rum-and-coke without a word. Bric peered at Brody's Mojito, cocked an eyebrow, and said with faux horror, "Off the hard stuff, I see. When did you quit soda?"

Brody didn't answer. Instead, he fished a creased envelope from his shirt pocket and nudged it across the bar. Bric set his glass down, cracked his knuckles, and tugged out the letter inside—a familiar fold of typewritten words. He paused midway through, sucked air through his teeth in a low whistle, and—after a thoughtful sip of rum—slid the letter back into its envelope and pushed it toward Brody. Both men sat in silence for a heartbeat, the hum of Hunks swirling around them. Finally, the elder Wahl spoke.

"She's right."

Brody bristled, "About what?"

Bric waved a languid hand. "About everything she said, and a few things she didn't. This little rock is too small, too quiet, too… mundane for a woman who's danced with Paris in springtime." He allowed himself a sly smile. "Between you and me, I'm surprised she stayed this long. You gave her two beautiful kids, sure—but she's too cultured to settle for a scuba bum."

"I'm not a bum," Brody snorted. "We've done fine— bank account's healthy, had a nice house outside of town until, well, you moved in and she moved out. Couldn't stand that big place alone, so I locked it up and climbed back aboard the houseboat."

Bric stood, stretched his wiry frame, and surveyed his son with mock pity. "Look at you—khaki shorts, a fishing shirt, Crocs that have seen better days, and I'll bet you haven't showered since your last dive rinse. Is that how you woo a princess?"

A voice from behind the bar—Montclaire, another old friend—snorted. "Or a queen, honey! I mean, camel-colored Crocs and purple—who dresses you, Picasso?" Kevin barked a laugh; Bric held up a hand. "Kevin, I'm having a serious father-son moment here."

Montclaire placed her hands on her hips, still smirking. "Oh, I know, dear. But you're talking to the camouflage Crocs guy. It's kind of endearing."

Bric turned back to Brody. "Remember when you first met Mallory—sand beneath her toes, sunglasses glued to her head, but she lived aboard a yacht. You were never going to measure up."

Brody gulped his Mojito, mint leaves swirling around the ice, then tilted his head. "Speaking of princesses—how did you manage to charm so many women? Spill your secrets."

His father laughed, a deep rumble that filled the space between them. "Secrets? I'm the biggest flop in history. I ran off your mother, got blocked by more women on Facebook than there are grains of sand here, and..." His voice cracked, eyes misting. "I never figured out the one I truly loved, Karen Murphy." He glanced at Brody's glass. "I sure didn't teach you how to drink. You learned that on your own. Why do you think you need lessons in chasing tail?"

Brody said nothing, just traced a circle in his nearly empty glass. He knew the advice was coming—his dad always had wisdom disguised as gruff talk. Bric closed his eyes, nodded once, and slipped into "professor mode."

"Getting laid," he said, "is like playing baseball. Bat .333 and you're a Hall-of-Famer; .200 and you're stuck in the minors. .100—well, you'd be swinging through vines and yelling like Tarzan, proud as punch at one hit in ten." He cocked an amused grin. "It's all about persistence—and three golden rules."

Brody flagged Kevin for a couple more drinks. "Three golden rules?"

Bric counted on his fingers. "One: Always be a gentleman. Hold doors, pay the tab, and yes, even if she's ten pounds heavier than you expected, don't mention it." He tapped his knee. "Sometimes 'gentleman' just means you support the conversation with your knees and elbows—properly, of course. Two: Never talk down or dominate. She's your equal. Listen more than you speak, even when she's waxing poetic about the sale on bananas at Winn-Dixie." He raised two fingers. "And three, most important: 'No' means 'no.' Tip your hat, pay the bar tab, say 'thank you,' and move on."

"That's it?" Brody asked, eyebrows raised. "Seems… simple."

Bric straightened, pressed a twenty onto the bar, and gave his son a steady look. "I'm no Casanova—I'm a disaster. Those are just my rules. Maybe it's time you write your own." He extended a calloused hand and pulled Brody into a strong hug. Then, without another word, Bric tapped his cane on the floor, navigated past a cluster of bikini-clad tourists, and climbed the narrow stairs at the back of Hunks toward his apartment, leaving Brody alone at the bar, his mind swirling more than the mint in his glass.

Seven Mile Bridge

10 Charley

Over the next month, my days fell into a ritual as steady as a metronome. Lilly and I lay tangled in our sheets until noon's searing sun had climbed high enough to heat the house. I would rise, steam from the shower fogging the tile, the scent of lavender soap lingering on my skin as I toweled off. Dressed in a crisp shirt and jeans, I slipped into my worn boots and slipped out just as Lilly clocked into work at two.

I started with errands in town—picking up sandwiches at the deli, slipping through the hardware store for what I pretended was household maintenance—before rolling onto US1. My unmarked white Ford cruised smoothly past the sheriff's office at Cudjoe Key; the deputies waved as I glanced in the rearview mirror, their smiles warm under peaked caps.

From there I threaded northward through Big Pine's sun-scorched palms, the slow curves of Summerland, the swaying mangroves of Sugarloaf, and on into Stock Island's cluttered docks before the neon blur of Key West swallowed me whole. I swept down North and South Roosevelt boulevards, circled Duval's tourists, drifted along Simonton and Whitehead, ducked into hidden lanes where the air smelled of salt and spilled rum. Each evening I checked in— "Nothing suspicious, sir"—and left the station light blinking unanswered. Weeks went by with no new bodies.

Then, one night, about two a.m., I was gliding past the Publix on Roosevelt when a stooped figure caught my eye. Under the flicker of a lone streetlamp, an elderly man tugged a small wire cart along the cracked sidewalk. I ducked under my visor, pressed the button that sent my portable red light clattering magnetically to the roof, eased the accelerator back, and let my siren chirp once, sharp and clipped. Rolling down the passenger window, I parked alongside him, engine murmuring, warm night air thick with humidity. I lifted my badge; he paused, peering through spectacles that caught the lamplight.

"Hey," I said, voice firm. "Dangerous to be alone out here. There's a murderer loose. He's targeting men just like you."

"I'm sorry, Officer," he replied, his accent soft and lyrical. "I was walking home from my dominoes game on Stock Island. I have no car."

"Next time get a cab," I scolded. Then softened. "Hop in. I'll give you a lift." I unlocked the rear door. "Put your cart back there."

"Gracias, Officer," he said, grinning. "I live on a houseboat behind Banana Bay—on Hilton Haven Drive."

He settled onto the leather bench seat, the springs creaking under his weight. "Chino Horowitz," he said, offering a gnarled hand.

I withheld the wild look of recognition. Charley Thomas, Florida Division of Law Enforcement—my badge name—met his soft grip. "Detective Thomas. I'm down from Orlando to track these killings. You've read the papers?"

He nodded. "Terrible. I pray for the victims and the killer each night." He laughed gently. "You know, there are more Jews in Cuba than folks think. I'm a true Jewban."

I shifted focus. "Walk much around here? Seen anything odd?"

He shook his head. "No, Detective. I walk to Winn-Dixie, to the barbershop, Old Town for work—I roll cigars by hand on Duval Street. I came over on the Mariel boatlift in the eighties."

I patted his shoulder; he flinched and then relaxed with a smile. I sensed he wasn't telling me everything. "Chino, want coffee at my place? I'll drop you off when I head back out."

His face brightened. "Sí, Officer. Thank you."

I texted Lilly—her number still fresh on my phone—and told her I had company. We drove through palms and hibiscus to her small stucco house painted pale mint. She'd wired the garage door to the visor; with a click we rolled in and the door sealed behind us. "Make yourself comfortable by the pool," I said. "Cream and sugar?"

"Mucho azúcar," he replied.

Good—sugar would mask the phenobarbital Lilly had already slipped into his cup. I slipped inside. Through the sliding glass I saw her crouched nude behind the couch, the moonlight flashing off her skin. I carried two steaming mugs on a silver tray—his in a red cup, mine in a green cup. The coffee's bitter aroma curled around us as we crossed the tiled patio.

The Latino sipped politely. We chatted—tales of cigar tobacco, neighborhood gossip—until I leaned closer. "Chino isn't your real name, is it? You were in trouble before?"

He stiffened. "Sí… I'm on probation." His speech thickened, words dragging as the phenobarbital claimed him. "My real name is Carlos… I made a mistake years ago. It was… innocent. I didn't know he was fourteen…" His last confession was an apology caught in trembling lips before gravity took him. He slumped from his chair with a soft thud.

From the darkness behind the sliding door, Lilly emerged—nude and intent—clutching a butcher's knife and surgical scissors, blades gleaming coldly in the pool lights. Together we heaved his limp form to the ground. I stripped him of clothes, tossed the pile into the firepit, and watched the gasoline flare crimson. His shoes and belt we bagged; his wallet Lilly insisted we keep.

I guided his inert body into the bubbling hot tub. He floated, arms splayed, as Lilly climbed in beside me. The jets hissed, filling the tub with oppressive warmth and steam. Lilly's nostrils flared; her pulse pounded at her throat. She leaned in and kissed his pale lips once, hard. I pressed his head gently into my lap as she gripped his flaccid flesh and, with one swift slice, severed what she desired. Blood spurted, turning the water a grotesque ruby. She watched, breath coming in quick bursts, slipping into a silent ecstasy that scarred my soul.

After ten minutes of silent carnage, I hauled him out onto the flagstone patio. Lilly, still trembling with dark satisfaction, helped me drag his body into the garage. I hefted him into the trunk, closed the lid on his emptiness, and stripped off my clothes for a long, scalding shower. Dressed again, I climbed back into the driver's seat and drove north on US1 under a sky that had forgotten stars. I waited until no other cars passed, then eased onto the shoulder and tipped his body over a bridge rail into the mangrove shadows, dropping his wallet on the road so it would be found.

How long can this go on? With Lilly's endless appetite and my stash of hillbilly heroin, I'm the fox in the henhouse—and I'm not ready to be caught. Nothing lasts forever, but for now, the hunt continues.

Wayne Gales

11 Brody

It had been several weeks since the shark- cage nightmare and the dismembered body when Brody's phone trilled insistently. Though the clock glowed 2:28 p.m., he was curled into a nap, sunlight slanting through the small porthole. Alongside him lay a sleeping woman—her pale blond hair fanned on a rumpled pillow, her nude form a living canvas of ink from skull-topped shoulders down through vibrant sleeves of roses and waves to her wrists.

Angel had tumbled into his world at Hunks the night before. Enough mojitos drank her up to a 'two' on his personal scale. Now her chest rose and fell in oblivious rhythm. Brody couldn't help but smile wryly: girls always looked better at closing time. He remembered his father's crack: "I've never gone to sleep with an ugly woman, but I've woken up next to a few."

The phone's caller ID blinked "Sands, MCSO." Brody hit answer. "Officer Sands. I figured you'd given up on me." "Grab your gear," came the clipped reply. "A motor unit's on its way in fifteen. Report of a body about four miles south of the Seven Mile Bridge in roughly twenty feet of water." Click.

Brody glanced at an empty Code Rum bottle on the counter—he'd sobered less than a day ago. If he called back, they'd find a less hungover diver. He dressed quickly, gathered his wetsuit, fins, regulator, and, before slipping out the door, he tossed three twenties across Angel's side of the bed—fare for her ride home, he figured, or whatever else she might need, and left. Anything truly valuable in the houseboat was safely under lock and key.

Ten minutes later, a gray sheriff's van rumbled up to the houseboat. The deputy behind the wheel offered no more than a curt nod. They drove in silence through a bleached seaside landscape to Marathon Marina, where Brody transferred his gear to the sheriff's patrol boat.

On the fifteen-minute run out to Moser Channel, Sands filled in the blanks. "Couple of spearfishers spotted the body at slack high tide in fifteen feet of water. Currents here run nearly three miles per hour on the incoming tide, so it might've drifted toward the bridge. If it's still shallow, scavengers haven't had a feast."

He pointed to an orange Safety Sausage bobbing lazily. "Start there. Take your time."

Brody moved to the bow and peered into the shimmering aquamarine depths. Each pass over the sandy bottom rattled his nerves until, on the fifth sweep, he shot a fist skyward. "There!"

The captain cut the engine and dropped anchor. Brody cinched his weight belt, clipped on his octopus, then rolled backward into the cool, particulate-filled water. He descended with slow kicks, the seabed rising to meet him in a haze of silt.

There it lay: a man's corpse, face down, limbs splayed. Crabs skittered across rotting flesh and tiny reef fish nipped at exposed tissue. Brody closed his eyes against the smell of decay, secured one ankle, then flipped the body to confirm his dread.

Moments later he surfaced, dragging the inert weight behind him. He tore off his mask, saltwater brine stinging his eyes. "Some critter already went Lorena Bobbitt on this guy's package!" he hollered.

Sands stood at the stern, arms folded, expression chalk-white. "'Another one,'" he said softly. "'That's five.'" The patrol boat drifted in the sunlit channel as though carrying the weight of secrets too grim ever to share with the press— or even the rest of Brody's dive team.

Wayne Gales

12 Charley

It was late afternoon when the phone finally rang, the sinking sun turning the walls of my living room a molten gold. The caller ID flashed "Monroe County Sheriff's Office." I set down my coffee, pressed a finger to my lips to hush Lilly on the couch, and offered a gentle "shh" as I lifted the receiver. My voice was steady, though my stomach twisted. "Monroe County Sheriff' s Office, Detective Halstrom speaking."

"Marathon Marina?" I murmured as I listened. "They pulled him from the water? Same mutilation?" I nodded, even though no one could see me. "I'm chasing a lead on Duval Street, but I can be there in forty minutes—just past mile forty-seven. Got it. Thanks." I hung up and turned to Lilly. " I need a quick shower and a change of clothes. I've got to go to Marathon."

She shot me a frosty look, barely masking her annoyance that our usual afternoon ritual would have to wait. "Sure," she said curtly, stalking off to the guest bedroom and slamming the door so hard the windows rattled. I sighed, knowing she was wrestling demons only she could face.

Ten minutes later I peered through the sliding glass door. Lilly sat by the pool in twilight's purple hush, wrapped in a pale linen sheet, a joint smoldering between her fingers. Smoke curled upward, vanishing into the humid air. I hesitated, then stepped onto the tile deck.

"C'mon," I said softly, arms open. "You know I've got to go." She didn't look up—just waved me away like a stray mosquito. I shrugged, turned, and headed for the garage, the engine's growl cutting through the evening stillness.

Crossing Seven Mile Bridge, the sky was bruised with clouds, and the wind whipped salt spray across my windshield. Traffic crawled in both directions; sheriff's cruisers ringed a section of guardrail halfway across, yellow tape fluttering like warning flags. I flicked on my magnetic rooftop light and gave the siren a single, piercing chirp. Cars parted before me as I motored to the scene.

Detectives knelt on the asphalt, swabs in hand, methodically combing the rail and road for clues. I flashed my badge—no one challenged me as I slipped beneath the tape. A deputy held a crinkled plastic evidence bag. "What've you got?" I asked.

"A wallet, Detective." He offered the bag.

I unsealed it, the plastic crackling. Inside lay a battered leather wallet, its surface slick with humidity. A handful of damp bills, several glossy business cards for a cigar stand on Duval Street—but no driver's license. Just a government ID: Carlos Horowitz, an address on Hilton Haven. I handed the wallet back. "Run him for records, warrants, anything," I said, already knowing there'd be little more than a parking ticket or two.

A few more minutes of highway brought me to Marathon Marina, where fluorescent lights swung overhead, illuminating tarps draped around the body. Florida Highway Patrol troopers held the perimeter, their polished boots tracing chalk lines on the concrete. Monroe deputies directed traffic, keeping gawkers at bay.

I spotted Jacob Sands elbowing his way through the uniformed ranks to hover near a somber-faced diver slumped in a folding chair, wetsuit still dripping. I flashed my badge at the troopers, then approached Sands as he peeled back one corner of the tarp.

The body lay face down on a portable gurney, pale and bloated from its time in the brine, limbs splayed at odd angles. Dark, jagged cuts at the neck and torso matched the grotesque signature of the previous victims. The air smelled of salt, diesel, and something coppery—blood.

"What did we find?" I asked, voice low.

Sands leaned in. "The diver brought him up early this morning. Same mutilation as the others. We've kept that detail close; no need to spook the public yet. Rumor is it could be someone on the force." His whisper was almost drowned by water lapping against the pilings.

My skin prickled. "What leads do we have?"

He shook his head. "Nothing solid. I've been checking hospitals and clinics—someone's missing a stash of phenobarbital. And we got trace DNA on two bodies, but only distant matches: fourth or fifth cousins, all long-time Key West residents." He tapped his clipboard. "Conchs, most likely. No criminal records to pull from."

I exhaled against the humid breeze. Sands managed a tired half-smile. "We're close. I can feel it."

I nodded, instructed the coroner to forward a full report, and slipped back into my car. The tarps billowed behind me as the marina lights faded in my rearview mirror. The Keys stretched out ahead—endless highway, endless questions.

13 Brody

The cell phone perched in its charger on Brody Wahl's nightstand trilled with the familiar strains of Darth Vader's theme through bleary speakers. He squinted through hangover-thick eyelids at the glowing red digits of the clock—1:28 AM—and groaned as he fumbled for the phone. "It's almost one-thirty," he rasped, voice rough, "you better not be calling just to say you love me." He paused, rubbing his forehead. "Also, I've polished off a few—okay, five— drinks tonight, so dive duty's off the table for the next twenty-four hours."

"Good morning, Brody," came the somber answer from his cousin, Detective Johnny Russell. "We're skipping the scuba gear. Another body turned up by the roadside at Mile Marker 19 on Sugarloaf Key, just past the high school."

Brody rolled onto his side, irritation flaring. "You mean to wake me from a perfectly good dream just to share that cheery news?"

"There's been a pattern. You've been on scene for the others—you might catch details we'll overlook," Johnny replied, tone mock-lecturing. "Remember, you're still on call with Monroe County Sheriffs. I'm calling you."

Brody groaned. "Give me ten minutes to shower. You picking me up, or do I drive so you can snag another DUI?"

"Fifteen," Johnny said. "I'll be at the front of the houseboat docks."

"Fine. And bring a peace offering—a large Dunkin' coffee with three sugars, three creams, and a maple bar."

They cruised up the Overseas Highway in near-silence, the sky a bruised purple at dawn. Brody cradled the steaming cup, the sweetness clashing with his cottonmouth. He replayed Jacob Sands's words: the detective was zeroing in on suspects, so maybe they were close.

Police lights bled red and blue into the darkness ahead. Monroe County Sheriff's and Florida Highway Patrol cruisers formed a tight perimeter around the scene. Brody and Johnny stepped into the harsh glare of spotlights, the night air thick with humidity and the faint tang of gasoline. Beneath a blood-tinged white sheet lay the body, face-down on the asphalt, officers murmuring in clipped tones.

Brody knelt and pulled back a corner of the sheet. "Look at those scrape marks down his back," he murmured. "He's bigger than the guy off Seven Mile Bridge—well over two hundred pounds. Must've taken hell to drag him out of a car. Bet that's why they dumped him here instead of over a rail."

A deputy shook his head. "No ID yet. Can't see anything in this light."

Johnny knelt too. "Gloves on, help me roll him."

Two deputies slid their hands under the corpse, the skin already stiffening, and turned him over. A collective gasp fractured the hush. Brody stared down, stomach churning. "Jesus," he whispered. "No shark took him on the roadside—and what's that in his mouth?"

Johnny's jaw clenched. "Jacob Sands briefed you? All victims have been mutilated identically."

Brody shook his head. "I thought the Seven Mile case was unique. He didn't have anything in his mouth."

"Could've washed away," Johnny said. "Or been picked clean by something."

Brody's voice dropped to a haunted whisper: "If Jake Sands ever needed evidence, it's gone now."

"Why?" Johnny asked.

Brody pointed, voice hollow. "Because this one…this is Jacob Sands."

14 Charley

"Find his ID?" I asked as soon as I stepped under the wavering yellow floodlight, already knowing the answer. The humid air pressed heavy against my skin. I'd reduced his wallet to ash myself before hauling the body out. Sand's badge lay at the bottom of the fire pit by Lilly's pool, a glittering lump of molten slag.

John Russell jerked his head toward his cousin in the shadows. "Not yet, but Brody is convinced it's Deputy Jacob Sands."

I offered a sympathetic nod, though inside I was seething at that cocky diver. I slipped on latex gloves and knelt beside the corpse, probing for familiar wounds. The man's uniform was singed, his face pale and drawn. "Same as the others," I murmured. "Where's the medical examiner?"

A young deputy checked his watch. "He's still in Miami. Told us not to move the body until he arrives—about four hours from now."

I sighed theatrically, eyes on the twisted metal pool ladder. "What a shame. I heard Sands was a damn good cop."

"A damn good cop," echoed a low voice. I glanced toward the pool's edge and saw Brody emerge from the darkness, droplets glinting on his wet jacket. He looked both proud and uneasy under the accusatory glare of the scene lights.

Rising, I peeled off my gloves and tucked them into my pocket. "You know the drill. Flag me down if you find anything. IDs are easier to spot in daylight." I checked the time on my Android. "I imagine you'll still be here when the sun comes up."

I started toward my car, then paused and turned back. "How did you get out here tonight? Your ride won't be arriving for a while." I lingered on his damp hair and broad shoulders. "Need a lift?"

Brody offered a half-smile. "Gee, thanks, Detective." He glanced back at the uniformed deputies milling around. "Don't mind if I do."

While he stowed his scuba vest in the trunk, I unbuttoned my blouse's top button and let the fabric part a little. Then I tugged my skirt up, revealing the dark sheen of my nylons and the edge of a garter strap.

He slid into the passenger seat, and I held out my hand. "Detective Charlotte Thomas, Florida Division of Law Enforcement. Everyone calls me Charley."

His gaze flicked between my décolletage and the flash of nylon at my thigh. "Pleasure's mine. Broderick Russell Wahl—Brody to most. Thomas—is your family from the Keys?"

"Ten generations," I replied with a warm smile. "Born and raised. A real Conch, through and through."

Brody's grin widened. "We might be kin, then. I've got Thomas ancestors on my mother's side. We should compare family trees."

I leaned forward, letting my blouse gape a little more, and exposed my legs well up the thigh.

"Great idea," I purred, and held out my hand. "Detective Charlotte Thomas, Florida Division of Law Enforcement. Everyone calls me Charley."

Then, as if I'd just thought of it, I added, "Before I drop you off, want to stop by my place for coffee? We can trace our roots over a cup."

"I'm pretty coffeeed out," he admitted, shifting in his seat. "But I could go for a rum drink—with the right company."

My hand drifted across the console to rest lightly on his thigh. "Why, Brody, I think that's an outstanding idea. I happen to have a fresh bottle of Bacardi in my cabinet."

His cheeks flushed as he leaned closer. "My favorite brand. Lead on, Detective Thomas."

I slipped my seat belt on and tapped out a quick text to Lilly. Then I let a private thought slip through my mind: *'Welcome to my parlor,' said the spider to the* fly.

Author's Notes

Somebody shoot me. As soon as I wrote my "last" book, people started asking me for more. Understand, I'm not documenting real stories, but making this drivel up one page at a time. Most of you have come to know Bric, Brody, Karen, Kevin (ah Scarlett), and even Stumpy, may he rest in peace, as if they are real live people. That's partly because every single one is fashioned after an actual friend, family member, or acquaintance. Some are perfectly portrayed, and some are composites of several individuals or stretched just a teensy bit. Brody is my son Matthew, large of body and an expert diver far beyond his years. Rumpy was my dear friend, John Stuempfig. We lost him a few years ago after losing his battle with multiple illnesses. He was my best friend, and I miss him every day.   His mannerisms, love of fishing, love of life, love of rum, and pretty blondes accurately portray him. Sail on, dear friend.

Karen is, well, Karen. A lifelong buddy from my days in the Keys, where we were both in the hotel business in sales. We traveled across the nation and around the world attending trade shows and conventions for nearly two dozen years, always representing different hotels and never on the same flights. Karen is now a hotel General Manager in South Carolina. We still keep in touch via Facebook.

Bric? Lots of people tell me when they read my stories, they hear my voice narrating to them. Fact: I lived in the Keys on a houseboat. I've traveled all over the world and played guitar in several bands over the years. I both frequent and love the various places in Key West featured in the stories. Fiction: I snorkel but am not a scuba diver. I've never been a Navy SEAL and have zero hand-to-hand combat experience. And if I had as many romantic trysts as Bric had, I would have either killed myself long ago or died of one of many communicable diseases.

Now, about *Bone Island Bodies*.

This story is a complete departure from anything I've ever written. For one thing, it's a novelette, longer than a short story and shorter than a novel. It's based on a short story I submitted some months ago when my former publisher asked if I had a piece about a Key West murder. I initially said no, then said "wait, give me two days," and then I cranked out a little piece called "*For Tillie.*" I shared it with friends & family and got a gamut of comments from "great job" to "sick bastard." I took the plot and massaged it into a novelette.

The other departure from my other books is that half of it is in first person, and half is written from third-person perspective. Briefly, first-person point of view is when the speaker refers to him- or herself. Third-person is the point of view where the author does not refer to themselves.

Sheesh, first a history lesson, now I'm teaching literature.

About The Author

Imagine a life lived to the fullest, a journey that has taken you from the thrill of professional motorcycle racing to the depths of the ocean in pursuit of long-lost treasure. A life where you've traveled the world, won awards for your culinary creations, and unearthed a rich family history that spans over a century. This is the remarkable life of Wayne Gales, an author, chef, and marketer who has lived a story worthy of his own novels.

Born with a taste for adventure, Wayne's wanderlust led him to visit all fifty states and twenty-three countries, immersing himself in diverse cultures and experiences. But it was his time spent in the Florida Keys that truly shaped his story. Living on a houseboat and closely following the narrative of the novel Treasure Key, Wayne found himself in the heart of the treasure-hunting scene, befriending local legends like Robert Moran, former Vice President of Marketing for Treasure Salvors, Inc. - the company responsible for discovering the legendary Atocha treasure.

These real-life encounters sparked Wayne's imagination and fueled his desire to write. Drawing on his experiences and the characters he met, Wayne began crafting the Bric Wahl series, a collection of eleven novels featuring a tough, soldier-of-fortune protagonist inspired by his own adventures.

Now settled in Melbourne, Florida, with his wife Tina, Wayne continues to write, bringing his vibrant story to life on the page. His work is a testament to the power of pursuing one's passions and the incredible journeys that can result from a life lived with courage and curiosity